CHARLES E. MARTIN

Island Winter

GREENWILLOW BOOKS · NEW YORK

Library of Congress Cataloging in Publication Data

Martin, Charles E. (date)   Island winter.
Summary: Staying behind on an island after
the summer people have left, Heather
wonders what there will be to do.
[1. Islands—Fiction]. I. Title.
PZ7.M356777Is 1984   [E]   83-14098
ISBN 0-688-02590-0
ISBN 0-688-02592-7 (lib. bdg.)

It was a sad day. Fall had come and the last of the summer people had left the island. Heather and her family stayed behind.

"What will you do here all winter?" Heather's friends had asked her. It worried her. She asked her mother.

"There'll be plenty to do," her mother said. "You'll see."

Wide awake that night, Heather looked out on a dark, cold island. The inn was a black shape against the sky. A little light came from a pale moon. Her parents were sleeping. Finally she went back to bed and slept until breakfast.

"This is the day I start building traps and painting buoys," her father said, "and I'm going to need your help."

"First things first," her mother said. "School starts tomorrow, and we have to get ready for that. Afterward, we will give you lots of help."

At school there was one big room with eight grades and eight children—three in the second grade, one in the fourth, two in the first, one in the sixth, and Heather was in the third. The teacher was Mr. Gray. His helper was Mrs. Gray. School was fun. Still, she thought about summer, about berrying in the woods, the picnics on Swim Beach, the busy store, watching the baby seals, and her summer friends.

That afternoon Heather and Kate and Sam raced their bikes and played games until dinner. On Saturday, at the fishhouse, she and her friend Alta painted buoys. Heather helped choose the colors. Father built traps and Mother brought sandwiches and they had a picnic.

The trees turned red and gold. Heather and the other children helped gather kindling in Cathedral Wood. Halloween came, and in art class they all worked on decorating the school for the Halloween party. At the party they dressed in crazy costumes, danced square dances, and ducked for apples. A big moon lit up the way home.

Heather and Kate took piano lessons and practiced on the school piano. Grandma and Grandpa came on the mailboat for Thanksgiving. Grandma said she was seasick, but Grandpa said it wouldn't hurt her appetite for turkey. It didn't. Everybody ate too much. The next morning was bright and sunny. They all took a ride inshore with Grandma and Grandpa. The sea was very calm.

For three days school was closed. The teachers had colds, along with three of the pupils.

It snowed, and out came the skis and sleds and snowballs. When school started again, Mrs. Gray reminded them that Christmas was two weeks away. She read them *A Christmas Carol* and asked if they would like to make a play out of it. They all said yes.

She also asked them to think about decorating the classroom for Christmas. Heather's drawings were the best in the class, and Mrs. Gray chose her to do the blackboard decorations.

Suddenly the temperature dropped. The pond froze—and there was ice in the water bucket. Heather got one of her presents early, a pair of shoe skates. Everyone skated all weekend. She fell 160 times, but she learned how to skate.

Back to school on Monday. Play rehearsals, school work, decorations, and just a little time to skate before dark.

The play was a great success. Heather was Scrooge. The applause
was long and loud. At night the island was bright with lights in every
window and there was a wreath on every door. Everyone got presents.
Toward evening on Christmas Day a heavy snow started falling. And
school was closed for a week.

It was skis, snowmen, sleds, shovels, and snowball fights, and it all
passed too quickly. New Year's Eve was a very quiet time on the island
because, very early on New Year's Day, lobstering began.

At gray dawn everybody came down to watch or to help the men set
out the traps. By early evening hundreds of different-colored buoys
bobbed up and down in the wintry sea. Everyone was tired and the
lights went out very early.

One warm day Mr. Gray took them to Swim Beach to hunt for arrowheads. Long before Columbus came to America, the Indians hunted wild ducks on the island. Everyone was excited when Sam found an arrowhead. It was a beautiful one and they gave it to the museum.

One fine Saturday Heather's father took her and her mother lobstering. They passed hundreds of buoys. They stopped at a blue and yellow one that Heather had painted and hauled in the trap. There were six lobsters in it. They threw back three—two tiny ones and a mother. They kept three big ones, plugged their claws to keep them from biting, and tossed them into a barrel. Heather's father baited the trap and put it down again. He took them back at noon and picked up his helper, Chris, and went out again. Did she like lobstering? Heather wasn't sure. Her father came home late and said they'd had a great day—and a great catch.

The ice cracked and melted in the pond and the gulls were able to swim and bathe again. Frogs sang and the wild geese honked overhead. Heather and her mother went to the cove to see two geese that had landed there, old tired ones, someone said, that needed rest before going on. They met some bird watchers from the mainland who carried binoculars and cameras and took lots of pictures. There were lights in the inn that night.

Houses were being painted and roofs repaired. More people came and they went about in groups, drawing and sketching, and suddenly it was June. It was warm and birds sang. Green shoots came out of the ground, Father dug a garden, and Mother put up new curtains. Strangers walked along the roads and the headlands. The boat came more often and something changed a little each day.

They knew school would be closing soon, and finally the day arrived. Everyone was promoted. One day the mailboat came carrying Barbara, their friend from New York, and two days later Ned and Jerry arrived. People were coming to open their houses. The boat brought lots of food and other supplies and the store stayed open longer. It was July.

"What do you do here all summer?"
Heather heard one of the newcomers say.